THE JOURNEY OF THE CRESCENT PENNY

CURT REYNOLDS

THE JOURNEY OF THE CRESCENT PENNY

Published by

Splickety Publishing Group, Inc.

www.splickety.com

ISBN 978-1-942462-17-0

Copyright © 2018 by Curt Reynolds

Cover design by Kirk DouPonce of DogEared Design

www.dogeareddesign.com

Available in print and ebook format on amazon.com.

All rights reserved. Non-commercial interests may reproduce portions of this book without the express written permission of the author, provided the text does not exceed 500 words.

Commercial interests: No part of this publication may be reproduced in any form, stored in a retrieval system, or transmitted in any form by any means—electronic, photocopy, recording, or otherwise—without prior written permission of the author, except as provided by the United States of America copyright law.

This is a work of fiction. Names, characters, and incidents are all products of the author's imagination or are used for fictional purposes. Any mentioned brand names, places, and trademarks remain the property of their respective owners, bear no association with the author or the publisher, and are used for fictional purposes only.

Scripture quotations are taken from the KING JAMES BIBLE/KJV, which is public domain. All rights reserved.

Library of Congress Cataloging-in-Publication Data

Reynolds, Curt

Journey of the Crescent Cent, The/ Curt Reynolds 1st ed.

❦ Created with Vellum

*For Jesus,
My Lord and Savior.*

1

Rural Iowa, 1940

Jacob eyed the baseball mitt and ball enviously. No one noticed.

He glanced at his mother, who continued strolling through the general store, carrying a wicker basket lined with burlap.

Every now and then she would pick up an item, lean a bit closer to the price, sigh, and then place it back upon the shelf.

Jacob picked up the ball. The new leather felt stiff against his skin. He put the ball back and ran his fingertips over the new glove, also firm to his touch.

He thought of the mitt he had back at the farm. It had been his father's when he was younger. A bit too big for his hands and cracked and faded with age. His father had insisted that a used mitt was better than a new one.

"It's got more experience than a new mitt. You'll learn faster with a mitt that's seen its fair share of a field," he'd said.

Jacob imitated his mother and checked the prices. $4.89 for the new mitt and ball.

He looked around the shop. The fully stocked shelves and tables contrasted with the scarce customers—just himself, his mother, and the shopkeeper behind the counter.

"Can I offer any help, Mrs. Woodland?" said the man. He was tall, taller than most, and sprouting a grey beard topped with a curled mustache.

Jacob's mother sighed. "Thank you, Orville. I think I've found everything this basket can bare." She approached the register.

Orville lifted the items out one at a time, handling each one delicately. The register clicked and ticked as Orville punched in their costs.

Jacob wandered up to the counter and stood at his mother's side.

She didn't look down at him when she spoke, but her voice was soft. "Are you wanting something, Jacob?"

He hesitated. "No, mama."

She nodded.

Gears wound, and the register bell dinged. "That'll be $2.39."

Jacob's mother opened up the cloth purse and handed Orville two dollars and fifty cents. Orville reached out with her change and dropped the coins into his mother's hand.

One of them slipped away, clattered to the wooden counter, and rolled toward Jacob.

He stopped the penny with an index finger and caught the flash of a year—1910. Sliding it to the edge, he pinched it with his thumb and handed it back to his mother.

The coin jingled into her cloth bag, a small and shallow metallic ring.

"My wife was hoping you would be in today, Mrs. Woodland."

Jacob's mother smiled. "I hope Helen is well."

Orville returned her smile, but his was partially hidden beneath his impressive mustache. Jacob wondered how old he had to be before he could grow a mustache like that.

"She's very well, thank you. She was wondering if you'll be attending the pie contest on Saturday night."

"Oh, yes. I've been looking forward to it. Is she entering this year?"

Orville stood even taller and smiled. "With my mother's recipe. Though, we know the judges are a bit partial to Mrs. Rollins's caramelized peach."

Jacob stopped paying attention. Pies didn't concern him much. Home runs and fly balls and perfecting his curveball—now *those* were topics worth talking about.

He could just imagine himself in the outfield,

catching a pop fly and getting the third out in the final inning. Their team would win, chanting and cheering his name. The crowd would go wild. No old, cracked mitt could do that.

"Jacob, aren't you going to answer him?"

He snapped back to the present moment. "Sorry, mother. Answer what?"

She frowned down at him, but a smile played at the corners of her mouth. "Orville asked how old you are now."

"I'll be nine next month, sir."

"Quite a growing man, then." He said. "Helping your father much on the farm?"

"A bit, sir."

Jacob's mother placed her hand gently on his shoulder. "Perhaps it's time he starts doing a bit more?"

Orville smiled and Jacob did his best to return it, but the thought of more work wasn't a pleasant one.

His mother folded up the burlap lining of her basket, securing the contents within. She said farewell to Orville, and together they left the shop.

Out on the main street, the town was busying itself with commerce. Women and children walked the sidewalks, bundled in heavy coats against the April chill. Men in suits wandered in groups of two or three.

Jacob overheard their discussions of work and news. He caught the flash of a newspaper headline announcing that the New York Rangers had won the Stanley Cup.

His mother looked up, and Jacob followed her gaze. The center square clock tower read 2:53.

"Judy? Judy!" Called a woman's voice.

Jacob and his mother turned toward the voice. A woman, maybe ten years older than Jacob's mother, bustled over to them. She carried her own basket, and Jacob noticed a paper sack of sugar inside.

"Hello, Marge. How're you this afternoon?" Jacob's mother said.

Marge looked a bit pink in the face. It contrasted with her loud shock of red ringlet hair. Her voice was always set to a pitch appropriate for shouting over a steam train. Jacob found that quite strange.

"Oh, it's just wonderful!" Marge bellowed.

Jacob noticed a few people across the street looking up to find the source of noise, and upon seeing Marge, quickly diverted their gazes.

"I've just finished my shopping for the big event on Saturday." Marge waggled her basket a bit. "Are you entering, too? It's been so much work!"

"No, I'm—" Judy started.

Marge interrupted her. "Oh, that's a shame. But less competition for me! I've been practicing for weeks! The sugar ratio is just so hard to nail down. Sometimes it's too little. Sometimes it's too much. You'd think a balance would be easier to find!"

"Yes," his mother started again, "that does sound—"

"I've made so many pies in the last week, I think my

husband will need a new belt! I'd better get this ratio down soon, or I'll run out of peaches."

Jacob looked around, desperately hoping for an escape from Marge's ramblings. He settled for daydreaming about baseball. He could listen to Marge all day if only he had a new ball to toss around.

"—get going. Best of luck, Judy!"

"Goodbye, Marge," his mother said.

When Marge was a sufficient distance away, Jacob asked, "Is her hearing okay?"

Judy laughed. "Goodness, that would explain quite a bit, wouldn't it?"

The clock tower began to chime. Jacob counted three tolls.

"We'd best scurry home." His mother added in a lower tone, "Especially before she comes back."

A chill accompanied the wind as they made their way south on 4th street. Near the edge of town, they turned left and headed out toward the country.

Soon the paved roads changed to packed dirt. And where there was business and commerce in town, outside those lines were freshly upturned fields. The smell of churned dirt and wet grass hung in the air.

They didn't talk much on the hour-long walk home. In the distance, Jacob could see his father riding the tractor they'd bought last spring. He was tilling the earth in the front of their farm, making the land ready for planting. Jacob hoped they'd have a good crop. A good crop meant an easier winter, and winter was always unpredictable.

Their modest house had two floors, three bedrooms, and four happy residents—Jacob, his mother, his father, and Jacob's best friend, Max.

She unlocked the heavy wood front door and he followed her inside.

"Put some water on the stove, Jacob?" His mother set the basket on a table in the entryway and removed her coat. She took his and hung them in the hall closet. "I'll take care of putting these items away and then start on dinner."

Jacob set off into the kitchen and fulfilled his mother's request, but their water bucket was getting low. It would need to be refilled at the well. Still, he got enough into the pot and set it on the stove to boil.

Jacob returned to the hall closet and retrieved his coat again. His mother was somewhere else in the house, putting away their purchases. Bundled up, he got the water pail from the floor of the kitchen and set out the back door.

Max, Jacob's golden retriever, came bounding up to greet him. He was easygoing, loyal, and didn't drool too much. It had always been Jacob's job to keep Max trained and well-bathed. And since Max loved nothing more than antagonizing the neighbor's cattle, he vacillated between relative cleanliness or being completely covered in mud at least twice a week.

"Tired of the fields?" Jacob asked.

Max looked up with a panting, canine smile, his tongue lolling out to one side.

Jacob took the pail by the rope handles and held it taut between his hands. "Okay, boy. Carry!"

Max took the handles of the pail between his teeth, and together they set off for the well.

It wasn't too far—just to the other side of the barn. Max tagged along, huffing and sniffing as they went. Around the corner of the barn, Jacob saw the well. And his father.

"Max."

Max was a distance behind him, antagonizing one particular hen with a game of chase that the poor bird clearly wanted nothing to do with.

"Max!"

Max ran up and looked at Jacob expectantly. Jacob took the pail from Max's mouth. Then he fully rounded the corner.

"Out here to get water for your Ma?" his father asked. He was sweating, despite the chilly April temperature.

"Yes, sir. She'll be fixing supper soon." Jacob said.

Hi father nodded and wiped his brow. "You get your lessons done?"

"Yes, sir. This morning. Then Mother and I went into town this afternoon."

"Oh? How was that?"

Jacob lowered the bucket into the well. "Fine, I suppose. We bumped into Mrs. Rollins."

His father laughed but caught himself. His face turned more serious. "She talk to your Ma about the contest on Saturday?"

Jacob nodded. "She talked a lot."

His father swore and looked down in embarrassment. "That's farm talk. Don't go telling Ma I said that."

"No, sir."

"Was she bragging about her pie-making?"

"Yes. How come Momma isn't entering this year?"

His father frowned. "We ate up all the canned fruits over the winter. You know harvest was hard last year."

"They've got fruits down at the store. Couldn't Ma buy some of those?"

His father's frown deepened and he pointed a dirt-coated finger at him. "Get your water, and get inside. And don't you say a word about that contest to your Ma, understand?

Jacob looked down at his shoes. "Yes, sir."

His father stood a little taller. "Buying fruit." He scoffed. "You didn't ask your Ma about that, now did ya?"

Jacob pulled hard to bring the water pail back up from the well. "No, sir."

All hope he'd had of telling his father about the mitt and ball was gone now. It might as well have been down at the bottom of that well.

Dejected, Jacob walked back toward the house. Max kept him company.

"And tell your Ma I'll be in soon!" his father called.

Jacob looked down at Max and discovered he was carrying his old baseball.

"Give that back!" Jacob yanked it out of his mouth. Max ran excitedly, clearly hoping Jacob would throw it. "Not a chance. This is the only one I've got. And it'll be the only one I'll ever have, too."

2

Jacob brought the filled pail into the house and poured it onto the bucket. His mother stood at the stove.

"Thank you for getting this started."

"Welcome." His voice was low with hurt, but he didn't care if his mother knew. He held up the old ball, still damp from Max's mouth. "I'm going to put this in my room so Max can't get it again."

He didn't wait for his mother's reply. Jacob sulked from the kitchen, dragging his feet as he went upstairs. At the landing, he turned left into his open bedroom.

It was simple. A small bed stood in the corner, and a chest of drawers sat at its opposite. A rug adorned the floor, and a wooden nightstand sat next to the bed. Jacob chose the chest of drawers to keep his ball safe.

He opened the top drawer. In addition to clothing, he

kept newspaper clippings. He had one about the Yankees beating the Cubs in the 1938 World Series, another about the Yankees beating the Reds in the 1939 Series, and various articles about Chicago Cubs players, past and current.

He sighed. It would be a dream to go to Chicago and see them play at Wrigley Field. But here he was, stuck on an Iowa farm with a happy dog that chewed his baseball and living a lifestyle too broke for fresh fruit.

He left the drawer open and sat on his bed for a while, still holding the ball. He tossed it up into the air and caught as it came back down.

He wondered when the Cubs would win the World Series again. They'd been losing since 1908. But a 32-year streak had to come to an end soon. As he continued tossing the ball, he wondered what it would be like to be in the crowd, cheering the Cubs on to victory.

Lost in his imagining, he missed catching the ball, and it clattered on the wood floor. The ball rolled to his dresser. Jacob got up and tucked it safely next to the newspaper clippings. He shut the drawer and returned downstairs.

The kitchen brimmed with tempting smells. His mother was busy making meatballs, mashed potatoes, beans, and mushroom soup. Jacob would've been happy without the soup, but he knew better than to complain.

"Go set the table, please," she said.

Jacob obeyed, and when he finished, he returned to the kitchen.

"Father is outside, washing up," she said. "I think we're all going to have a little talk over dinner tonight."

"About what?"

"You."

"Me? Did I do something wrong?"

She smiled, teasing him. "You'll have to wait and see. And by the by, thank you for bringing in more water. That was very thoughtful."

"Sure. Should I light the candles?"

His mother glanced out a window. The sun was setting now, and the darkness of night grew stronger. "Yes, I think so. These electric lights are hurting my eyes. Turn on the radio, too? Some music would be nice."

Jacob set off. He used the fire in the stove to light a long match, and soon the dining room glowed from hardy candles. The radio took a little fine-tuning, but at last he got it to play.

The raspy sounds of recorded brass flooded the room. It was a slow waltz, some tune Jacob didn't recognize without the lyrics.

His mother came into the room. She carried half empty platters of food and set them on the table. Jacob went back to the kitchen and helped her finish.

Just as he set the last one on the table, he heard the back door open and shut. For half a second, he heard a groaning and recognized Max's familiar whining.

His father appeared in the doorway. "I know this one."

"Hello, dear. How was your day?"

His father smiled wide and swept over to his mother. He gathered her into his arms and dipped her low for a kiss.

Jacob rolled his eyes and looked away.

"Moonlight Serenade," his father said. "I love this song."

Jacob went into the kitchen. He turned off the lights and did his best to ignore the giggly sounds coming from the dining room. At last, when it seemed the coast was clear, he entered.

His father sat at the head of the table with his mother on his right side. Jacob pulled out his chair and sat opposite of her.

They all held hands as his father said grace. As they began to dish up their plates, Jacob's father initiated the conversation. "I saw a buck while I was out in the fields this morning."

"Really?" Jacob said. "Was it close?"

"It stayed on our land for a bit, but then it wandered north, toward the Johansens' property. Perhaps Gary saw it, too."

"We went into town this afternoon." His mother ladled out meatballs from a bowl.

"So I heard," said his father. "How did that go? Did you see Helen?"

"No, she wasn't about." She passed the bowl over to Jacob. "I did see Marge."

His father rolled his eyes. "I'm terribly sorry."

"She means well. She's just not very... sensitive."

"Or silent," said his father. He cast a glance at Jacob, who immediately looked down to his plate, smiling to himself.

"Apparently they have so many left over peaches that she's been practicing for Saturday's competition for weeks."

"The meatballs are very tasty, Mama." Jacob said.

"Thank you, dear." His mother smiled warmly at him. "Jacob brought in more water earlier, dear."

"Yes, I saw him out at the well."

"Ah." His mother's mouth curled into a wry smile. It was the same look he'd seen when they had left the shop earlier. "He also saw a new baseball mitt and ball while we were in town."

"Did he, now?"

Jacob's stomach dropped and soared and dropped again. How had his mother known? Had she caught him looking at the prices? He hadn't asked for it. She'd even asked if he wanted something, but he's said no. Was he in trouble for it? He knew there wasn't money to spare for extra things like that. No matter how wonderful and new they were.

His father cleared his throat. "And how did that go?"

"Quite well," his mother said. "He didn't ask for them.

He also didn't think I saw him looking." She smiled at him. "A mother knows everything."

Jacob blushed and looked back at his supper once more. With a spoon, he began playing with his soup. He'd tried to get the broth and avoid the mushrooms, but he hadn't completely succeeded.

He heard the rattle of coins. His mother still wore the little purse at her waist. "I didn't think much of it until he brought in that water without being asked. He'll be a young man of nine next month."

Jacob's father nodded, his gaze shifting between Jacob and the coin purse.

His mother addressed him first. "I'll be honest Jacob, we simply can't afford a new mitt and ball for your birthday."

Now his father blushed.

"But you've been proving lately that you're leaving some aspects of childhood behind and entering into a new phase of life. Not adulthood, no. But it's high time you learn a few more things around the farm. We'll continue your lessons, but in the afternoons—if your father is agreeable to it—I think you should join him out on the land. For this, we can begin giving you compensation. Does that sound agreeable to you?"

Jacob nodded fervently.

She smiled. "Good. Then, here." She reached into her bag and pulled out a coin. She paused for a moment, studying what she held. After a moment, she placed it on the table and slid it over to him. The copper scraped noisily against the wood. Jacob reached and took it.

It was a penny. Or it was supposed to be a penny. There must have been a mistake when it was minted. The image of Lincoln and the year 1910 were still visible, but the entire design had been shifted down and to the left. The top right hand side was just smooth, untouched copper in the shape of a crescent moon. It was unmistakably a penny, but a highly unusual one.

"Is this real?" he asked.

His mother nodded. "I think it's perfect. That penny will help remind you of the value of saving and of the wisdom offered in Proverbs 21:5. If the mitt and ball are what you want, then you can learn to work a bit more and save up for them. How does that sound?"

Jacob looked to his father, hoping for his approval as well. He smiled and nodded.

"I will," said Jacob. "Thank you. This means a lot to me."

Perhaps if he worked extra hard, he could save up enough to buy tickets to a game at Wrigley field. That would be worth even more that a mitt and ball. He'd need to find out how much it would cost to go, and to eat, and to stay in the city.

But Jacob's day dreaming was interrupted by a knock at the front door. His mother and father exchanged a look.

"Who on Earth?" she asked.

His father wiped his mouth with a napkin and stood from the table. "I'll go and see."

His footsteps were loud as he crossed the room and went into the entryway. The bolt on the door slid back, and the door creaked as it opened.

"Gary!" His father exclaimed. "Please, come in."

"Terribly sorry for calling at such a late hour, Robert," said a gruff voice. Mr. Johansen came into view. He was a few years older than Jacob's father. More grey streaked his hair, and the laugh lines on his face ran deeper. Under his arm he carried a package wrapped in butcher paper. "Good evening. How do you do, Mrs. Woodland?"

"I'm very well, thank you. This is a pleasant surprise, Gary."

Jacob's father returned from shutting the door and stood next to Mr. Johansen. "What can we do for you?"

"Are you hungry? We have plenty of food on the table."

Jacob chanced a glance. Hardly anything remained.

Gary smiled. "No, thank you. I've already eaten. I had my day interrupted by a stag."

Jacob's father laughed. "Is that so? I think I saw him crossing my line over to yours."

"That was the one. I got him with my rifle. He was huge. Too huge for our ice box, even." He held up the paper wrapped parcel. "So I thought I'd come by and see if you wanted to add a bit of venison to yours."

Jacob's mother looked delighted. "That's very generous of you! Are you sure you have extra to spare?"

"Oh, yes," he said. "Better to share it than let it spoil. After all, when you have more than you need, build a bigger table, not a bigger barn."

His mother stood to accept the package and take it into the kitchen. But Jacob caught the look in her eyes. And she wore the same, devious smile he knew so well.

After a few more pleasantries, Mr. Johansen headed back to the door. Jacob's father went out with him. He didn't say so, but Jacob suspected they were going to enjoy a pipe out on the porch.

His mother sat down at the table. She was smiling, her eyes full of light. She looked lost in thought.

"Mother?" he asked. "What are you up to?"

One corner of her mouth turned up. "There is no rule in the contest that the pies must be of a sweet variety."

"So..." Jacob started.

Her eyes flashed once more. "I think a fresh venison meat pie is exactly what that contest needs."

3

Jacob didn't place the penny in his piggy bank immediately. Instead, he kept it in his pocket, sort of as a good luck charm.

By the end of the week, he had earned eleven cents around the farm. Eleven hard-earned cents. His days started early with his father and were interrupted by his school lessons with his mother. Midday meant going back out onto the land. And by the time supper rolled around, he was exhausted.

But it was all going to be worth it. A new mitt and ball were his for the earning.

When Saturday rolled around, he still helped his father in the morning. But come mid-afternoon, it was time for everyone to wash up and get ready to go into town. His mother left hours before he and his father were ready. She carried with her basket filled with flour, salt, sugar, shortening, an egg, an onion, a potato, and a choice cut of the venison.

Jacob watched from the window as she left, her head held high. She didn't have the extra supplies to practice the pie for weeks on end. But he could see determination in her stride as she left the farm.

A few hours later, Jacob sat on his bed, looking at his nightstand. A glass piggy bank sat on it. It was still empty. Eleven cents in the form of one nickel and six pennies stood stacked next to it with the crescent cent on top. He knew he should be saving them.

But the pie contest was bound to have all kinds of vendors and games. He'd worked hard all week, and it seemed a shame to attend it empty-handed.

He swiped the coins into his pocket.

The walk into town with his father was considerably shorter. His father took long, quick strides, and Jacob struggled to keep up at times.

When they reached town, it was even busier and more alive than it had been midday Tuesday. Cars lined the streets, and groups of people wandered up and down the shops. Most folks seemed to be headed in the general direction of the dance hall.

Outside the hall stood a wooden sign:

PIE CONTEST TONIGHT
50 CENT ENTRY
$10 PRIZE

Jacob paused by the sign. He could see whole families headed into the hall.

"Your mother is quite ingenious," he said. "Just hope her harebrained idea doesn't rub folks the wrong way."

Jacob smiled. He thought his mother's plan was brilliant. It was certainly making the best of a hard situation.

Inside, the hall was alive with music and laughter. Long tables had been set up, topped with pies and labels. Many women stood behind their pies, smiling and offering tips to passersby. All in all, there must have been at least forty entrants for the contest. The hall was alive with the music of several violinists playing in one corner.

As Jacob expected, several vendors had set up booths around the edges of the room. The largest of all was the Rollins Bakery.

They were selling pies, pastries, bread, and cookies. On their sign hung nine blue ribbons. Jacob assumed they were the ribbons Marge had won with her famous peach pie.

The stand was attended by the Rollins daughters—three girls with curly blonde hair, all between the ages of eleven and fourteen. A whole pie was 15 cents. A slice was only a nickel.

The stage was set with a table and five chairs, one for each of the judges. Jacob wasn't sure who two of the judges were, but he recognized Mr. Lorrensby, the mayor, and Mr. Rollins, the town baker.

It seemed a bit unfair. It made sense to have him as a

The Journey of the Crescent Penny

judge, Jacob supposed, but to let his wife compete and win every year was as bad as mixing up sugar with salt.

"Let's find your mother," his father suggested.

Jacob agreed. But as he scanned the room, he didn't see her anywhere. He hoped nothing had gone wrong. He doubly hoped she hadn't backed out of her idea. His father spotted Helen, and they went over to her.

Helen had made a classic apple pie. "Hello, Mr. Woodland. How are you this evening?"

"Quite well, thank you. How's your husband?"

"Orville is happier than a pig in mud. He's down at the shop. Keeping it open late tonight."

His father nodded. "Have you seen Judy anywhere? I expected her to be here."

Helen smiled wide. "Oh, yes. She came over to our home. Baked her pie there not even an hour ago. She's likely still there." Helen winked. "It's a fantastic idea, you know. I just hope it's enough to knock Marge off her high horse."

"We'll find out," he said.

"She's already paid her entrance fee." Helen the table on the space next to hers. "She'll be right here when she arrives. Don't fret. She'll be along."

Jacob looked around the room. No sign of his mother yet. But the youngest Rollins daughter caught his eye. She smiled and waved for him to come over.

"Papa, he said. "I'll be right back."

Jacob worked his way through the crowd, bumping

against elbows and doing his best not to trip anyone. He stood at the booth, and the youngest daughter leaned over the counter.

She had huge blue eyes, round and sparkling. They reminded him of a doe. He looked around for his mother once more.

"Hi, Angelina."

"Hello, Jacob," she said. "Here to see us win another year?"

He wrinkled his nose. "I wouldn't be so sure. My mother is entering."

"Oh? And what did she make?"

"I don't think I'm supposed to say."

She leered at him playfully. "A secret, then? Well, well. Tell you what. I'll give you a whole pie for only ten cents and that little secret. How does that sound? So long as you don't tell my sisters."

He rooted around in his pocket and produced the seven coins. The face of the crescent penny stared up at him. The smooth copper caught the light of the hall and reflecting white orbs on its surface.

He remembered again why his mother had entrusted him with more chores and why he was working so hard at the farm. He took ahold of the nickel and slipped the other coins back into his pocket.

"Just a slice, please," he said.

"Are you sure?" She winked and played with one of the blonde curls that cascaded down her shoulder.

"Yes, ma'am. Just a slice. I should be getting back to my father."

She pouted but handed him a slice on a plate with a fork. "Five cents." Her face scrunched into a scowl as he handed her the nickel.

"Well... bye, then," he said.

She pouted some more.

Jacob wandered away and found his father again. He came upon his father, still lingering around Helen. His father raised an eyebrow at the pie in Jacob's hand.

"Best finish that before your mother arrives." He reached out to the plate and smiled. "In fact, I think I better help." His father took a bite of the famous peach pie. "She's not winning for nothing. It *is* good."

Just then, the host came onto the stage holding a microphone. "Welcome ladies, gentleman, and young ones. I hope you're all enjoying yourselves. It's time to start the judging of our contest! Could I please have contestant numbers one through eight join our judges on the stage with their pies?"

"I'm number 18," said Helen. "Judy will be 19. We've got a little while before they call us."

"She needs to be here soon," said Jacob.

His father folded his arms. "Will they still let her be judged if she's not here on time?"

Helen looked around the room. Fret lines etched her face. "I'm not sure. I doubt it. Could be seen as an advantage."

His father glanced at the stage, where Mrs. Marge Rollins was dishing out a slice of her pie to the mayor while smiling at the fifth judge, Mr. Rollins.

"Well, we wouldn't want the competition to be *unfair*," his father said.

Jacob searched and searched for his mother. The crowd made it difficult to see, but so far, he hadn't spotted her. The eighth contestant was leaving the stage.

The announcer resumed his spot and said, "Attention! Could I please have contestants nine through sixteen join us on stage with their pies?"

"Maybe I should go and find her," Jacob said.

"Maybe *I* should go and find her," his father echoed.

Jacob set out to search the crowd and return the plate to the Rollins Bakery stand. He approached it with caution—not quite tiptoeing, but not taking confident strides like his father, either.

Peeking around the corner, he saw the youngest sister and oldest sister busy with something at the back of the stand.

"Hi, Jacob," said the middle sister. She had the same curly blonde hair, but was a little rounder in the face. "Can I help—"

"Nope!" He dropped the plate and fork onto the counter and darted back the way he came.

By the time he reached his father and Helen again, only two contestants were still onstage. His mother's group was next.

"Having trouble with the Rollins girls?" Helen asked.

His father shot him a glance.

"No, ma'am." Jacob lied.

Helen rolled her eyes at him. "Oh, look!" She pointed toward the door. "There she is!"

Jacob's mother came rushing through the door, carrying her pie in both hands. She stopped at a table near the front and filled out her label card. The woman seated at the table raised an eyebrow at Jacob's mother.

But she proceeded without issue. His mother had been right. Savory pies weren't against the rules.

She came over to them and set her label card and pie on the table. The edge of the crust had been lovingly pinched and folded, rippled perfectly.

Several slits in the top of the crust made a swirling pattern. Without question, it was the best-looking pie in the room—to Jacob's eye, at least. Her card read "Farmer's Fortune."

"Just finished it," his mother said. "Wanted to make sure it would still be warm when the contest starts."

"You're just in time, Judy," Helen said. "Our group is being called next."

His father leaned over the table to inspect the pie. "How did it go? It looks incredible."

"I think it's my best yet. We'll find out," she said.

The host stood at the microphone once more. "Okay, folks. Let's bring contestants seventeen through twenty-four on the stage."

Helen and his mother picked up their pies.

His mother leaned in for a kiss from his father. "Wish me luck!"

Jacob watched as they lined up at the stage. He could see the anticipation lingering on his mother's face.

Suddenly the weight of the peach pie weighed heavily in his stomach like a stone. Guilt racked him, and he shifted back and forth, one foot to the other.

What if she lost to that peach pie again? She'd be crushed.

His heart wrenched in pain as she stepped up to the judges.

4

One year later...

Jacob sat in his bedroom, his gaze on his glass piggy bank. It contained the fruits of his labors, and it was nearly full. He hadn't kept track of its contents. He wanted it to be a surprise.

But as the June sun poured through his window, the call of a new mitt and ball was too strong. He reached for the piggy bank and shook it over his bed. It took some time, getting all the little coins to line up with the slot and pour out.

A mountain of metal sat on his bed. He organized it into groups of ten cents. By the end, he had totaled it all up to $5.82.

The new mitt and ball cost $4.89. He'd had that price memorized for ages. And he checked it every time they visited the general store.

Finally. I finally have enough.

Pride and excitement swelled in his chest. He couldn't wait another day. He couldn't wait even another hour before he went into town.

He rushed downstairs and found his mother in the kitchen.

"Ma," he said. "Do you have an extra coin purse?"

She looked up from kneading dough. "Of course, dear. What do you need it for?"

A huge smile conquered his face. "I've got enough saved. I want to go into town and get my new mitt and ball."

She nodded. "Check the hall closet. There should be one up on the shelf. Let me clean off my hands. I need a few things from the store as well. I'll give you a list and money for it. I just don't have time to go into town today."

"How's the preparation coming along?"

"Quite well, thank you." She nodded to her apron where last year's blue ribbon was pinned. "I'd like to have a matching pair, but there's no venison this year. So we're making a go of it with rabbit."

"Sounds perfect." Jacob ran out to the hall closet and found the spare purse. Then he darted up to his room and filled the purse with all of his coins. Holding it in his hand, he couldn't help but notice it was roughly the same size as a baseball.

When he reentered the kitchen, his mother had

readied a list. She tucked it and her own purse into her usual shopping basket. "Straight there and back, okay?"

Jacob nodded. "Okay."

"And..." She paused. Her eyes welled up. "I want you to know that I'm proud of you. 'The plans of the diligent lead to profit.' You've really embodied that over the last year."

"Yeah, thanks. I guess so."

He kissed his mother farewell and set off for town.

Summer sunshine warmed his skin. Only a few wisps of clouds marbled the sky. A breeze graced his face as he made his way down the old, familiar road. He spent the walk lost in daydreams, imaging the feel of a new ball in his hands.

The town was busy. Jacob kept his gaze to the sidewalk, not wanting to bump into anyone. Conversation held no interest for him. Not now. He made a direct path to the general store.

The bell above the door chimed as he entered the shop. It was warm, and the smell of wood and fruit wafted through the air. A few other shoppers milled about the store. A young woman loitered near the shoes. A little girl, younger than Jacob, clung to the hem of her mother's skirts. Jacob saw the look of envy in her eyes as she stared at the shoes.

He headed for the back of the store, where the toys were kept.

Ready to make his purchase, Jacob reached for the mitt and ball.

"Mama," the little girl said. "Can we look?"

The small voice made him remember that his own mother had sent him with a list. He quickly pulled it out and gathered up all the things she needed.

He placed them in the basket and kept his mother's purse on top. Peeking into the purse, he saw that she'd sent him with quite a bit more money than what he needed for those items. At least an extra six dollars.

He returned to the back of the store and picked up the baseball mitt. It was light brown with a single strap between the thumb and forefinger. The leather was supple, smooth, and completely uncracked.

It didn't have so much as a wrinkle. The ball was almost pure white, with vibrant red stitching. It fit perfectly into the palm of the mitt. Jacob couldn't help but smile.

Anxious to hurry home, he carried the basket, mitt, and the ball to the counter. Orville stood behind it, and a man Jacob didn't recognize stood off to the side making notes on several pieces of paper.

The mother and young girl were making their purchase of a few necessities. Jacob noticed there wasn't anything fancy or frilly about their clothes. If anything, they looked a bit sun-worn and thin. The daughter carried a new pair of shoes.

That must be nice, he thought. *Just asking for something and it's given to you.*

Pride swelled in his chest. He had worked hard to earn this mitt and ball. He deserved them.

The little girl placed the shoes on the counter. She was barely tall enough to see over it. She pushed them as close to Orville as she could.

"Wait," the mother said. "How much is our total without the shoes?"

Orville leaned over slightly and checked the register. "$5.76"

The mother held out seven dollars in paper bills.

Orville frowned. "I'm sorry. Those shoes are three dollars."

"Please, sir?" the child asked.

"Anna," the mother hissed. She turned to Orville. "Times are hard. Is there no way to make this work?"

Orville's frown deepened, and he shot a glance to the unknown man lurking nearby. "I wish there were. But times are hard for everyone, even for a shopkeeper. I'm sorry. I wish there was more that I could do."

The mother nodded stiffly. "Just the other items, then."

"But Mama…"

"We'll talk at home, Anna. Okay?"

The disappointment on the girl's face was obvious. Jacob felt sorry for her, but the mother should have kept better track of the cost before promising new shoes to her daughter.

The woman paid for her other items. Jacob watched as Anna's lower lip quivered. She tilted her head up, trying to stop her tears from falling.

Then Jacob saw the shoes Anna currently wore. The laces were new, but rest of them... They looked older than his baseball mitt—cracked and with several holes at the heel.

She must've been wearing them for a long time. Her toes bulged causing the leather to stretch and discolor. Her feet were squeezed into them.

The mother took Anna's hand as they turned to leave.

Before they reached the door, Jacob heard her whine. "But these hurt, Mama."

The shop door bell tinkled.

"Can I help you, Jacob?" Orville said.

"Yes." He placed mama's basket and items on the counter.

Opening her purse, he remembered all the extra money his mother had sent with him that day. His mother was a charitable person. If she'd been there, surely she would have offered to buy the shoes for the little girl with her money.

Her money. That was his mother's money, not his. He didn't have any claim to spend it for her. Even if she wasn't upset, it would break her trust.

He remembered how brokenhearted she'd been

before the silly little pie contest last year. Yet as rough as their times had been, Jacob always had what he needed.

He set the mitt and ball on the counter and ran his fingertips over the smooth leather once more. One last time.

He almost said he didn't want them. "I won't be buying this." He glanced over to the shoes. "Please let me buy those instead."

"The... the shoes?" Orville raised an eyebrow. "Are you sure?"

"Yes. And quickly? I'll come back for my mother's items."

As Orville rung up the shoes, Jacob poured out his change onto the counter. Once again, he stacked it, although with a bit more haste this time.

As he finished, he noticed the crescent penny in the group. He froze for a moment, transfixed by the year. 1910. For a moment, he almost replaced it with a regular one.

It had been the start of his journey and had served as a reminder to him over the last year. A reminder of the importance of keeping promises. He smiled. He'd learned the lesson.

It was time for that little penny to move on.

"That will be $3.18"

He pushed the change over to Orville. The crescent penny shined atop the pile.

He reached over the counter and grabbed the shoes.

"I'll be right back!" He rushed outside.

Anna and her mother had made it about a block and half up the street.

"Hey!" Jacob cried out. "Wait! Anna, wait!"

They didn't turn around. Maybe the mother didn't think he was calling out to *her* Anna.

Jacob broke into a run, both of the little shoes gripped tightly in his right hand. He continued calling after them.

At half a block away, they finally turned to look back.

It was clear that the mother saw Jacob first, but Anna spotted the shoes. He slowed down to a jog, and Anna came running up to him. Her mother trailed behind her.

Anna's hopeful little eyes looked up at him.

"Hi," he said to her. He turned to her mother. "Hello." He looked down at Anna and held out the shoes. "These are for you."

Immediately, Anna took them from him.

"Wait, honey," her mother said. "Young man, we can't accept them. I... I don't even know you."

"Please do. I've been earning money for doing chores around our farm. I was saving it up for... something special." He looked at Anna.

She sat on the ground and began tearing off her old shoes. Her feet were noticeably larger than the old pair.

Jacob looked back to her mother. She watched as Anna anxiously laced the new shoes. Conflict contorted her face.

Jacob spoke again before she could object a second time. "This is much better than what I had in mind."

"Are you sure?" the mother asked. "I can't repay you for this. Nor can I thank you enough."

Jacob nodded. "I'm sure. This is what I want."

Anna stood and pranced around him. She gave him a farewell hug. Her mother gave Jacob a final, wary glance, then Jacob turned back to the general store to finish his mother's purchase.

He had made a difference, even if it was small.

5

For the most part, Jeff had finished his business with Orville. He watched as the young boy left carrying a basket. The baseball mitt and ball still sat at the end of the counter. Jeff left his papers where they were and picked up the mitt and ball.

"I'll put these back, then?" he said to Orville.

Orville nodded. "That was a bit odd, wasn't it?"

Jeff shrugged. "Kids."

"How are yours faring?" Orville said. The bell of the front door chimed again. A young woman, unattended, wandered around the front of the shop.

Jeff looked her up and down. She was tall, thin, with long brown hair kissed with streaks of auburn.

"Oh, they're just fine," he said.

"And your wife?" Orville asked.

Jeff turned his back as he restocked the unpurchased items and rolled his eyes. "She is well also."

He watched the woman make her way through the store. She stood on the opposite end of the shop as the register near a small bookshelf. Well out of earshot of Orville. Jeff pushed his left hand into his pocket and approached her.

"Hello, there," he said.

She looked up at him with large eyes, deep brown with an alluring hint of green.

"Are you finding everything alright, Mrs. ...?"

"Ms." she said with a quick smile. "Ms. Larron."

"Ms. Larron, my name is Jeff Anderson. It's a pleasure to meet you. How do you like the selection here?"

"Oh, just fine." Her sigh suggested otherwise. "My family moved here not long ago from the Des Moines area. Shopping there was a bit more... diverse."

"Des Moines, you say? What a small world. I'm based out of Des Moines." He admired the youthful glow in her face. She had a warm, welcoming smile.

"A small world indeed," she replied. "The selection is fine, although I do miss the wider range of book choices." She gestured to the novels on the shelves next to her and lowered her voice to a whisper. "I don't think anyone around here has even heard of Susan Ertz."

Jeff certainly hadn't. "Her work is fantastic. You enjoy it?"

She nodded.

"Well, perhaps when you return some day, you'll find the selection more to your liking," he said with a wink.

She smiled pleasantly and politely returned to her browsing.

Jeff returned to the counter and reviewed his papers once more. "I think I have just about everything you'll need for a restock, Orville," he said. "But how about a few more books? I hear great things about an author called Susan Ertz."

Orville shrugged. "Novels aren't a popular seller here, Mr. Anderson."

"Ah," said Jeff. "But Mrs. Ertz has a very loyal following. Why not give it a try?"

Orville raised an eyebrow at him. "You're the expert here. I suppose it wouldn't hurt."

Jeff made notes to have a few Susan Ertz novels added to the shipment. "Well, I think that about does it."

The shop's bell rang, and Jeff watched with disappointment in his stomach as the lovely Ms. Larron left.

"I hope the trip was well worth it," Orville said. "It's a long way to come."

Jeff shrugged. "Only four hours. And it was, thank you. I picked up a new contract with the Rollins Bakery as well as the Hickory Diner. Business is finally getting back on track these days."

Orville nodded somberly. "It can be hard going for some folks, as you saw."

"Well, I won't take up much more of your time," Jeff

said. "Although, I do think I'll take a soda pop and candy bar for the road."

Orville nodded. As Jeff shuffled his papers back into his briefcase, Orville set about grabbing the requested items. "That will be eleven cents, Mr. Anderson."

Jeff handed him a dime and a nickel. Orville pulled four pennies from the cash drawer and closed it again. As Jeff took his change, he glanced down at the coins.

"Huh." He held out one of the coins. It must have been misprinted. Most of the image of Lincoln remained, as well as the year 1910. But part of the penny was unstamped. It reminded him of a waning moon. Smooth, untouched copper shined up at him in a crescent shape.

He thanked Orville, and with a tip of his hat, soda in-hand, candy in-pocket, and briefcase tucked under his arm, he left the shop.

Out on the street, he looked up and down for any sign of Ms. Larron but found no trace of her. He headed to his car and steeled himself for the long drive home. Perhaps another day their paths would cross again.

6

Jeff went to work early the next day. In part, he wanted to get a jump on settling the new contracts, and also in part, it enabled him to leave the house before his wife awoke.

Over the last day, Ms. Larron had preoccupied his mind. She reminded him of his wife, 20 years ago. Before children, and a mortgage, and more children. Before age and worry had changed her looks.

Jeff couldn't rightly say he was unhappy, only that it seemed that something was missing. She'd been so fun once upon a time. Now it seemed everyday cares dragged her down in a way he couldn't understand.

He entered the office and hung his hat on the coatrack in the hall.

"Mr. Anderson?" called a bulky, rasping voice.

Jeff walked down the hall to Mr. Bronson's office. He

sat behind a large oak desk, his feet propped upon it so that the leather soles of his dress shoes faced Jeff. He wore a bowler hat, and a cigar smoldered in an ashtray at the corner of his desk. Luke Bronson was at least 15 years his senior.

"Come in," the man said. "Take a seat. I was just reviewing the contracts you dropped off last night."

Jeff chose the chair in front of the desk situated closer to the door. "Is there a problem, sir?"

"A problem?" Mr. Bronson raised one eyebrow and examined Jeff from above the papers. "Not at all. This is fine work."

"Thank you, sir."

"While you were away, I reviewed some of the other towns and contracts in your file. Do you know what I found?"

"No," Jeff replied honestly.

"Growth." Mr. Bronson placed the papers on his desk and swung his feet back down to the floor. Leaning over his desk once more, he resumed smoking the cigar. "Everywhere you go, there's an average of 37% sales growth. New contracts. Expanding on old ones. This is exceptional."

"Thank you, sir," Jeff replied. "And if I may be so bold, I hope you'll keep that in mind when my annual raise comes around in November."

Mr. Bronson chuckled. "If you're still here, you mean."

Jeff stalled a gasp. "Sir?"

Mr. Bronson took a long pull from the cigar and exhaled a plume of smoke. "While you were away, we received word from the main branch in Chicago. They have an open position for a regional director of sales. I think you should apply for it—with my highest recommendation of course."

Jeff was taken aback. Pleased, but a bit shocked. He fidgeted with the fabric of his trousers around his knees. "That's very flattering, sir. But I doubt I'm qualified for that. I've never even held a management position, let alone to become a regional manager."

Mr. Bronson shook his head. "Nonsense. Managing is all about being good with people and being a good worker. You've got a great abundance of both."

"Well, thank you, sir." A plethora of questions ran through Jeff's mind all at once. He settled on the most practical. "Where would it be located, sir?"

Mr. Bronson pulled on his cigar again. "In Chicago, of course." More smoke poured from his nostrils.

"That's a good ways away. I would need to run this by my family."

Mr. Bronson chuckled. "You haven't got the job yet." He pointed a sausage-sized finger toward Jeff. "But you'd make double what you're getting here in the first year alone."

"That... that is something to consider, for certain. All the same, this would mean a relocation. I'll need to consider their desires before I even apply for it."

Mr. Bronson nodded. "Well, a man who thinks of his family first shows wisdom. That's a good, biblical quality. Tell you what: Competition will be stiff for this position. I'll handle these contracts today. Why don't you take the day off, go home, and speak to your wife about it. Come in tomorrow, and we can move forward from there. How does that sound?"

Jeff considered it, nodding slowly. It was, after all, a windfall opportunity. But he would have to go home and...

Well, he couldn't avoid that forever.

"I think I will, sir. Thank you."

"Happy to help, Jeff. I like to see upstanding men like you achieve their highest potential. The good Lord only gives us one life to live, you know."

"Indeed, I do." His gaze fell on the contracts. "One thing sir, on the order from Orville's General Store, could you make sure the most recent books by Susan Ertz are placed there? Orville has had a special request, but I'm not readily familiar with that author."

Mr. Bronson nodded again and took a few quick puffs from his cigar. "Sure, sure. Anything they need."

Jeff excused himself from the office, his step lightened by Mr. Bronson's compliments. He donned his hat, and set off back to his car. Parked two blocks away from the office, he lost himself in daydreams of Chicago and maybe even an office with a view of the city.

"Hello, Mr. Anderson," said a deep, young voice.

Jeff pulled himself out of the daydream. He smiled at the young man that had addressed him. "How do you do, Henry?"

Henry was young. Young enough that he still should've been in high school. Yet every day, Jeff found him on this street corner or else another one nearby peddling newspapers.

He had a boyish grin, and the few blond whiskers on his face betrayed that he couldn't grow a beard or mustache.

Henry nodded. "I'm well, thank you."

"And how is your mother?"

"She's doing all right. The doctors are putting her on a new medication next week. Say she's become too tolerant of the current one."

"Is that to be expected?"

Henry frowned and shrugged. "Seems like they don't know much about it. Every time they fix one thing, it causes something else. I'm beginning to think they don't know half of what's wrong with her."

Jeff shook his head. "That's a real shame. I'm sorry you're both going through this."

Henry smiled, but the gesture didn't reach his eyes. "We'll get along one way or another." He cleared his throat. "Would you like a paper today, sir?"

Jeff smiled. "The usual, please."

Henry took a paper off of the stack. "That'll be five cents."

Jeff rooted around in his pocket and pulled out some spare change. He noted again the off-center penny. For a moment, he wondered if it counted as real currency or if it might be more valuable due to the error.

Perhaps some previous owner had thought so too. Despite being 30 years old, it looked freshly minted. He settled on a nickel and placed the rest of the coins back into his pocket.

Jeff and Henry exchanged the paper for the nickel.

"And where's my riddle today?" Jeff asked.

Henry smiled. "Are you ready for this one? It's a real stumper."

Jeff straightened his vest. "Let me have it."

"Mary was born on December 25th, but her birthday is always in the summer. How can that be?"

Jeff laughed. "Well, she lives in the southern hemisphere, of course."

"You're too sharp, Mr. Anderson. Too sharp. But I promise, tomorrow's riddle won't be so easy."

Jeff laughed. "Tell you what. You stump me with a riddle, and I'll give you all the change in my pocket."

Henry stuck out his hand and Jeff shook it. "You've got yourself a deal."

Jeff unfolded the paper and scanned the front page. The British and Free French forces had invaded Syria. "Whole word has gone apey. A second world war."

Henry shook his head. "Just lucky we haven't been dragged into it I suppose."

Jeff nodded. "Last thing we need is a great big expensive war. Folks are finally recovering from that depression. Last thing we need—mothers sending their sons overseas."

Henry looked off into the distance as though he was seeing beyond the buildings and city. "Still... to get to see the world. And on Uncle Sam's dime. Doesn't seem like a half-bad way to live."

Jeff raised an eyebrow at him. "Don't you go enlisting until this whole thing is over. Your mother needs you here."

Henry frowned.

Jeff's stomach lurched. He knew he'd said exactly the wrong thing.

He stammered, trying to backpedal. "I only meant... These are unknown times, Henry. Pastor says we're living in the end days. All that Hitler nonsense and whatnot."

Henry nodded slowly, but his jovial nature hadn't returned. "I knew what you meant sir. No offense taken."

"I am sorry," Jeff said. "I didn't mean anything by it."

Henry waved his hand. "Don't worry yourself over it."

Jeff bade him an awkward farewell and returned to reading the paper as he walked back to his car. Inside, he tossed the paper onto the front passenger seat and sighed. Hands on the steering wheel, he rested his forehead on the back of his fingers.

He had to go home. He had to face his wife. But now

he'd expunged the joy and excitement of the possible promotion with that one thoughtless comment to Henry.

He sat up again and steeled himself for the task. He was a salesman, after all. He could win her over on this.

Couldn't he?

7

Jeff pulled into the driveway, took the key out of the ignition, and waited in the car for a few minutes. He looked at the front window. The curtains were still drawn.

Lynn likely didn't know he was home yet.

He read the paper for a bit. He checked his watch. He'd been sitting there for at least twenty minutes. He read the paper a bit more.

Once half an hour had passed, he decided he'd delayed long enough.

Still, he hesitated at the front door.

Finally, unlocking it with his key, he stepped inside.

"Lynn?" he called. "I'm home." He began hanging up his coat in the closet. He entered the living room, but he still saw no sign of Lynn. He called out for her again.

"Jeff?" she answered from another room.

He set off through the house, down the hallway, into the study.

Lynn sat at the desk, penning a letter. She turned toward him. "Honey, what are you doing home this early?"

She rose and kissed his cheek. He made a small attempt to return it but landed mostly on air. She wore a simple dress that covered most of her frame.

She smiled at him, and the wrinkles around her eyes and mouth deepened. Even so, he still found her brown-and-green eyes beautiful.

Then his mind went to Ms. Larron. He couldn't help it.

"Is something wrong?" she asked. "Is it something at work?"

He shook his head. "Nothing is wrong." He peered over her shoulder, peeking at the letter on the desk. "What were you writing?"

"Oh, just a letter to my sister. I still can't believe she and Anthony moved all the way to St. Louis. It's so far away."

He frowned. This didn't bode well for the topic he needed to discuss. "That was over two years ago."

She looked crestfallen. "And I haven't seen her once since then. Not on a holiday or a birthday. It's just so sad. She's missing out on seeing her nephews grow up. And it's such a big city."

"You have five other sisters, Lynn."

She recoiled. "That doesn't make her any less important to me. I think she let herself get talked into it." She shook her head, disgusted.

He nodded, unsure how to approach the possible promotion.

"Something is bothering you," she said. "What's brought you home so early? It's not even lunch time yet."

He motioned her over to the loveseat. She sat beside him, her body turned toward him, engaging. Her knees brushed his. Perhaps he had missed her. A bit.

"There's an opportunity at work. A position has come open. A regional director of sales. It would pay double what I'm currently making."

He watched as she processed the news. Lynn kept the books of their house in order. He knew she would value an increase in lifestyle.

"How does Mr. Bronson feel about this?"

"He approached me with it. He's giving me a full recommendation for it."

"Well, Jeff, that's wonderful! Of course you should apply. You've worked so hard. You deserve a promotion."

He nodded and broke eye contact.

She withdrew a bit and folded her arms across her belly. "There's something you're not telling me."

His gaze fell upon the letter at the desk, and hers did as well.

"What? Does this have—no." Her eyes snapped up to him. "It's not in Des Moines, is it?"

"No," he confessed. "It's in Chicago."

Mouth agape, she was too stunned for words. A moment passed. Her chest rose and fell, gradually becoming higher and faster. She took in one deep breath and exhaled. "That was very deceptive of you."

"What was deceptive of me?" He folded his arms.

"Telling me it was a promotion, and double the salary. You essentially asked for my permission without—"

"I did *not* ask for permission."

"Oh, so you're what? Going to just up and move us to Chicago without even consulting me?"

"I'm not moving to Chic—"

"But you're thinking about it!" She stood and put distance between them.

"I wouldn't do it without *talking* to you first. And we're talking now."

She shook her head, no longer facing him. "You went about it the wrong way. You should have been up front with that little *detail*. My entire family is here. The boys' school is here. *All* of our friends are here. Why would you think we could just start over in a new city, all of sudden? And Chicago is *huge!*"

"It would be a great opportunity for us. It would be... it would be an adventure."

"And *adventure?*" She mocked him. "We're nearing *forty*. What do we need with adventures?"

All at once, his avoidance of her, reading the paper in the car, his approach in telling her—it all felt entirely justified. "Yes, an adventure. It would be fun. Are we too old for fun?"

"Fun? I have bridge with the ladies. I let you go to the pub with your friends, and I never complain. Do you know what the other wives in my group say when their husbands do *that*?"

"Yeah? Well, you should hear what we complain about in the pub. Then you'd understand why we have to blow off a little steam. What would *you* have to complain about, anyway? *I* haven't changed in our marriage." Jeff regretted it the moment he said it.

Lynn's cheeks flushed, and tears streamed down her face without her blinking.

Her voice came out as a hoarse whisper. "So, that's what this is? You want an adventure because your wife is old? Round and wrinkled and no longer fun? You resent me for how I've had to change for our family, for *us*?"

He tried to approach her, to comfort her. "No. That's not what I meant. I'm sorry I said that."

She backed away and wouldn't let him touch her. "You said it because some angry part of your heart *means* it."

"I'm sorry, Lynn."

She moved closer to the door, one hand outstretched to stop him from approaching or speaking. "I don't mind you getting a promotion. And I certainly don't mind your income increasing. But I will *not* move away from my family. It would break my heart." She stood silent for a moment. "Speaking of bridge, the ladies are coming over tonight. I'd prefer if you weren't here."

She left the room.

Jeff sank back into the loveseat. Had his bitterness gotten out of control? Was she right? Did he really hold that in his heart?

Sure, women like Ms. Larron were enjoyable to talk to. But... had he really crossed that line? Resenting his wife...

How could he come back from that?

8

He lingered in the study. Shutting the door, he picked up the phone. By two o'clock, he had alternate plans for the evening.

He knew it would anger Lynn. But she'd gotten upset over nothing. He hadn't at all meant what she had said. She was jumping to conclusions. That was her fault.

She got to keep up her social life. Why couldn't he maintain his?

He busied himself about the kitchen, making himself a late lunch. It was difficult and awkward given that Lynn was preparing food to serve at bridge. They managed with gruff "excuse me's" and "behind you's" and "Sorry, need that's".

He informed her he that would not be in the house that evening, as she had so nicely *requested*. He neglected to mention where he would be. She didn't ask, either.

The Journey of the Crescent Penny

He spent the rest of the day in the living room, reading the paper. He read it cover to cover, or at least the parts that interested him. Soon the clock on the wall read 3:12.

He reread the paper again.

At 3:42, he got up and laced his shoes, put on his hat, and shouted goodbye from the front door. He didn't want the boys to see him angry. He'd see them tomorrow. They'd have schoolwork anyway.

Stepping outside, he shut the door behind himself. His fingers lingered on the doorknob for a moment. He let his grip loosen, and he headed for the car.

The drive to the pub didn't take but perhaps twenty minutes. It was still early, hardly after 4:00 according to his watch.

He headed to their regular table and waited for his friends to arrive. A server stopped by and took his order. They had four brews on tap. Jeff chose the lager.

It was 4:45 when the first of them came trickling in. Ernest and Willard were roughly the same age, but impossible to confuse for one another. Ernest was thin, long legged, and his bowler hat hid no hair. The men often joked that his wife used it as a mirror when they were out.

Willard was stout, shorter than average, and had a head full of dark curly hair. Strangers were always surprised to hear that they were brothers.

Kevin arrived ten minutes later. He was dressed head

to toe in working clothes. June was prime construction season. He had a hard squint and calloused hands.

Lastly, Jim entered. Lugging a briefcase at his side, he wore a gray suit and somber, burgundy tie. His salt and pepper hair was neatly slicked back with a harsh side part with not a strand was out of place.

He joined them at the table. Although last to arrive, Jim initiated the conversation.

"This feller dropped two men and injured a third at a filling station in the north west side, and the jury just came back with a split decision."

The waitress stopped by and dropped off his a usual —whiskey on the rocks.

Jim continued, "Gonna have to start all over again."

"That's a tough break, Jim," Jeff said.

Ernest and Willard nodded along.

Jim just shook his head and sipped.

Jeff turned toward Kevin. Jim had a habit of oversharing, especially in those murder cases. "How's the construction going, Kev?"

Kevin smiled. "Weekends of overtime. Working twelve or fourteen hours a day. Gotta eat in winter, though, so I can't complain. Molly wants to send the twins to clarinet and piano lessons. They don't pay from themselves."

Jim cut in. "Those are good things for girls to have. Men like women with musical talent."

Kevin shot him a skeptical glance. "They're only nine.

I got some time before those grey hairs sprout, and I gotta get the old shotgun out."

The men chuckled.

Ernest leaned in, and even the low light of the bar reflected on his scalp. "Speaking of talented women..." He shot a glance back to Willard.

Willard smiled. "We got a new secretary." He shot a meaningful glance around the table.

Jeff thought of the job in Chicago.

Kevin laughed. "She a looker?"

Ernest smacked the table with his palm. "Is she ever!"

"Spill it, boys, spill it!" Kevin said.

Jeff leaned back in his chair. Hadn't Kevin just been talking about his daughters—his brilliant twin girls that he shared with his wife?

But then... *Ms. Larron.*

He shook off the thought with another sip of lager.

Ernest clutched just above his heart and went into details. All the men nodded. "Can't be more than twenty-four."

Kevin shook his head and stared off into the distance. "I remember my wife from those days."

Jim joined in. "Who doesn't? Barb hates my hours."

"And my business trips," Jeff added. A sharp pang stabbed his stomach.

Willard nodded. "She doesn't want me to stay in the office late. But she hates it when I bring work home. Well, which way do you want it?"

"Exactly!" Jim agreed.

Willard continued on. "And what does she have to complain about to begin with? The bills get paid, and we've got one of the nicest homes in the neighborhood. What more does she want?"

Jim shook his head. "They want everything. They want you there at the house, but don't get under their feet. Don't stay too late at work, but bring home enough bacon to feed all her friends for their parties."

Jeff thought of Lynn, likely at home and having a very similar conversation to this one. He hoped not. He didn't want the boys to overhear their mother speaking of him like that.

His stomach panged again. No, that wasn't it. He hadn't been fair to her. Or kind. He knew it.

He took a long drink. There were few things Jeff hated more than being wrong.

Jeff hung around for the evening as the men bantered back and forth. Women, wives, kids, bosses, houses, and what their neighbors were buying to outdo them.

The conversation droned late. He chimed in when he had to. But the pain in his stomach made it clear what he had to.

He only hoped he wasn't too late.

9

Once again, Jeff's fingers lingered on the front doorknob of his house. All the cars had left by this hour. It was after eleven. Her turned the key and pushed open the door.

The house was quiet. Jeff shut the door behind himself. He hung his hat in the closet and kicked off his shoes.

"Lynn?" he said to the silent living room. There was no evidence of a girls' evening. No errant plates or dishes abandoned on the coffee tables.

He went down the hallway and entered the kitchen.

He saw her then, just in time to not turn on the kitchen light.

Illuminated by a single lamp in the corner. She was fast asleep on the dining table. Playing cards sat in a neat stack in the center. He glanced to the sink. The dishes were washed and drying on the countertop.

Lynn. So responsible.

He stepped over to the table and soundlessly slid out a chair. He sat and looked at his wife.

Her head rested on the crook of her elbow, face pressed into her forearm. It wasn't a flattering angle. It plumped her cheeks and highlighted all the wrinkles that hadn't fully formed.

He looked at her with a critical eye and tender heart.

Which of the wrinkles had started during the rain on their wedding day, or when the bakery had gotten their names wrong on the cake? Which ones came from the car accident he had a year later and spent a few days in the hospital with a broken leg?

She'd gained weight from the pregnancies. All three of them. Which of her age lines had started when they lost the second baby at 18 weeks?

And now... Here they were. They had fought and struggled together to get this mortgage in this neighborhood, to get their boys into the best schools in Des Moines. They were in this together. Their little family... it was everything to him.

No, she wasn't young and perfect anymore. Age had changed her. He ran his fingers through his ever-thinning hair. Age had changed him too.

And shouldn't age have changed his heart as well? He

wasn't some carefree stag who could chase skirts and gams every weekend. She had changed for him. And if he was honest with himself, he hadn't changed enough of himself for her.

A part of him was still convinced that she existed to bring him happiness. But that wasn't true. *A husband must love his wife as he loves himself.*

Boy, how. He sure hadn't been doing that.

But he could change. He could do it now.

Gently, he placed a hand on her shoulder. She stirred and looked up at him.

She rolled her head back and forth as she sat up. "When did you get in?"

"About five minutes ago," he said.

"Listen, honey. I'm sorry I—"

He held up a hand to stop her. It was his turn.

"You were right to let me have it today. I knew what I was asking for was unfair. And I wasn't as honest as I should've been." He gripped her hand tighter and pulled it to his lips. He kissed the back of her fingers. "I'm going to do better for my bride. Can you forgive me?"

"Of course." She stood and kissed his forehead. "Let's go to bed. Morning comes early."

He rose and pushed in both of their chairs, and spare coins jingled in his pocket. The Chicago job was out of the question.

But that was okay.

His marriage wasn't in question.

Jobs were a dime a dozen in the end. His wife was one in a million.

10

The next morning, Jeff decided to skip going to the office early.

Instead, he got up and made breakfast for family, making sure to have all the dishes washed before the boys even left for school. He kissed Connor and Mike goodbye and then got ready for work himself.

In the hall, Lynn caught him before he could get his shoes on.

"Jeff, listen." She said. "I really do think you should apply for that job in Chicago. It's a good opportunity and—"

He cut her off with a wave of his hand. "I insist. The boys' school is here, all of our friends are here, and your family is here. It would break your heart to leave the Des Moines area. I can't do that to you. I'm happy in my work. And I'm good at it."

She scrunched her eyebrows down, like she wanted to argue with him. But she didn't voice any further concerns.

He wrapped his arms around her waist in drew her in close for a kiss. As he pulled back, he smiled at her. "Really. I insist."

Minutes later, he dashed out the door, fixing his hat as he sank into his car.

His mood was good... Right up until he realized he would have to explain to Mr. Bronson why he was turning down the offer. Hopefully it wouldn't be a bad conversation. But it would likely be uncomfortable.

Henry. Henry would have some advice for him. Or at least a listening ear.

Fifteen minutes later, he parked his car in town.

Henry occupied his usual corner and was already set up for the day. He sat on stool and called out to passersby.

Jeff called, "Hello, Henry."

Henry smiled and nodded at him. "Hello there, Mr. Anderson. How's your morning?"

"Jovial." Jeff allowed himself a wide smile. "But you know I can't go a day without the latest news.

Henry nodded and handed him a paper. Absentmindedly, Jeff began to flip through it, headed for the classifieds.

"Forgetting something today?" Henry asked.

Jeff looked up at him. "Oh!" He dug into his pocket to fetch the five cents.

Henry waggled a finger. "No, sir. Riddle first today. And you remember our bargain?"

"I surely do." Jeff smiled. "Okay, then. Let me have it."

Henry sat up a little straighter. "A man goes into a store and buys a pound of meat and a loaf of bread for $1.12. The meat was a dollar more than the bread. How much was the bread?"

Henry crossed his arms and leaned back, smiling like the cat that caught the mouse.

Jeff looked him up and down and shook his head. "Oh, now, Henry. That's not a riddle at all. The bread was twelve cents."

Laughter reverberated through Henry's body as he clapped and rocked back. "I finally got you, Mr. Anderson! I said the total was $1.12, and the meat was a dollar more, didn't I?"

"Well, yes," said Jeff.

"Now if the bread was twelve cents, then the meat was only eighty-eight cents more. No, sir. The bread cost six cents, and the meat was a dollar and six cents. That makes it exactly a dollar more. You see?"

Comprehension dawned on Jeff.

He smiled at Henry. "You... you got me. Well, I'm a man of my word."

He dug into his pocket and pulled out all of the change. There might've been nearly two dollars there.

And he noticed the penny, the shimmering 1910 crescent. He felt a little remorse in letting it go. It had been with him back in Orville's shop, and he'd carried it around in the days since. That little penny had seen a lot of change in a man's heart.

Henry's hand was outstretched.

But a deal is a deal. Jeff slid the money into his waiting palm.

He saw Henry's gaze fall and linger on the misprinted coin. But if he was going to investigate it, he saved it for later. Henry slipped the coins into his own pocket.

"And now that I'm utterly broke, I'd better get into work." He tipped his hat was on his way. As he walked down the street, he called back, "You stay out of trouble, you hear?"

"Yes, sir. I will!" Henry called back.

Jeff turned his attention to the paper. It was still folded open to the classified section. He shifted his fingers as he read and slowly walked to work.

There was an open position—tri-city director of sales at another general supply store. And it was based right out of Des Moines.

11

The mid-June sun shined as bright and hot as ever when Mama's illness took over.

Five days after passing out at church, she now took up a bed at General All Saints Hospital.

The doctors had moved her from one wing to another. Now she shared a room with a patient thirty years her senior. And Mama was the one in worse health.

Henry knew the doctors had tried. He'd seen them and the nurses working all hours of the night to try to save her. Henry had been there. He hadn't left since she was brought in.

Now his mama was flushed with fever and fraught with hallucinations, and there was nothing anyone could do to make her better.

He hated the pain medicine they put her on. But when she was awake, she hallucinated fires and men chasing her. At least with the medicine, she slept. He hoped they were peaceful dreams. She looked peaceful.

Once the doctors told him there was nothing else they could do, Henry resigned himself to keep her on the medication. She slept all day and night. She never woke up.

On July 1st, she passed away.

And Henry was alone in the world.

He had no one to take care of anymore.

The empty solitude was suffocating.

On July 3rd, she was buried. The entire church congregation attended the service.

Henry greeted them in somber tones. He'd worn his black suit—his only suit—to the viewing and the funeral. The church members kept him company. He was the first to grab the shovel and toss dirt on her casket.

Still, he was alone.

And somehow it was solitude he sought on his long walk home.

Others had offered to give him a ride their cars, but he wanted to walk. He wanted to think and to breathe and to see the ground passing beneath his feet. He wanted to make sure it was still there.

Hours later, he arrived at home. His grandparents had lived there, and his mother had grown up there. Henry had grown up in that house too. The stale odor of old cigarettes hung in the air.

He slipped off his shoes and put them in the coat

closet. His mother's fall and winter coats hung there, reminding him that he didn't know when she last wore them.

He went to the kitchen. The dishes had sat for weeks now. He'd made the last meal here. His mother had been too weak.

A stack of magazine and newspapers took up an entire cushion on the sofa. The other half of the couch was well worn and sagging. Those subscriptions had been a constant companion for his mother.

Down the hall, his mother's open bedroom was first. He averted his gaze and blindly reached for the doorknob. He shut the door, succeeding at not looking inside. He proceeded to his room and closed the door to change.

After it clicked shut, he realized he didn't need to shut it for changing anymore. He was the only one home.

He sank onto his bed and reached for a photograph on the nightstand.

It showed him, his father, and his mother. They'd gone on a fishing trip when he was twelve. It was the summer before his father passed away.

Henry proudly held up the twelve-inch trout his father had caught. His mother was laughing as his father leaned in to plant a kiss on her cheek.

He lay the picture face down on the nightstand. He was an orphan. He couldn't stand looking at them. They were smiling, happy.

None of the people in that photograph knew the

factory accident would happen to his father. None of them knew his mother would become terminally ill.

Now he was alone.

But every fiber in the carpet reminded him of her. Every scratch on the doorways, every rip in the wallpaper.

Henry remained behind.

But he couldn't remain there.

12

On the 4th of July, Henry set to work.

He gathered up boxes from behind grocery stores and shops. He packed up the house. Everything.

He'd resolved to keep one little shoebox of mementos and memories to remind him of the happiness that had once been there. It was all gone now.

It felt good to have something to do. But he detached himself from the emotions of the task. Dresses and shoes, needlepoints and playing cards. He boxed up everything from dishes to the old record player.

As the sun set that night, he looked around the house. Unless it was furniture or nailed down, he'd packed it up. A mountain of boxes sat in the middle of the room.

Henry wasn't sure what to do with them. Donate them, perhaps? There was enough in them to set up a family after a house fire or something, he supposed.

He liked the thought of his mother's belongings going on to help someone else. She'd had a caring spirit. He nodded to himself. Yes, that's what she would've wanted.

Henry slept in his bed that night. The handful of items he needed to get by were all piled on top of his dresser.

He liked it that way. It helped him organize his thoughts. Everything he needed was within reach. And he intended to live with a lot less.

The bills would start pouring in soon. Bills for the water, the gas, the electric.

His family had owned the home since before his grandparents had passed away. If not for that, he and his mother surely would've ended up on the streets when she got sick.

He got up and penned a letter to his Aunt in Iowa City. He explained his intentions and asked her preference.

He would sign the home over to her if she wanted, or she could sell it. He would split the profits with her 50/50. He wouldn't be around to sell it. She'd have to do that herself.

He was going to leave. He had to leave.

He didn't know how to live there anymore—in that house and in that city without someone to care for. In the first two days after his mother's passing, he wondered who would need him? Who could he take care of without her around?

The Journey of the Crescent Penny

Then something Mr. Anderson had said came back to him: *"Don't you go enlisting until this whole thing is over. Your mother needs you here."*

It was a callous comment at the time. But, in hindsight, it was thoroughly appropriate.

She didn't need him here, and he didn't need to be here.

But Uncle Sam? Not everyone agreed that they ought to get involved with that war. It might not even come to American shores, after all.

But Henry had read all the papers. He read them front to back, and he read between the lines. He knew it was coming.

Soon enough, Uncle Sam would need all the able-bodied young men it could find.

And Henry was going to answer that call.

He wanted to travel, not only to escape but also to explore.

And who saw the world more than the grand United States Navy?

They had stations all over the world. He'd read about them. And he wanted to see them.

He thought back to that day on the lake, the day when his father had caught the trout. The water had fascinated him then.

He was ready to set sail.

13

A week later, Henry strode into work at the Daily World a half-hour early for his shift. He had to see his boss.

As he stepped into the printing room, he clutched the papers under his arm a little tighter. To him, they were his most prized possession.

He stopped at the office door. The gold letters MS. HUDSON painted on the glass were now chipped and fading with age.

He knocked.

"Come in," she called.

He opened the door.

"Henry," she said, her voice soft and low, like she was speaking to her own child.

She was a thin woman, and taller than average. Despite the hot July days and the heat given off by the printing machine, she wore a long sleeve green dress with white lace at the cuffs and collar. She had a large hooked nose, and small rectangular glasses.

"It's good to see you," she said. "How have you been?"

He shut the door and sat in one of the wooden chairs across from her desk.

He nodded, taking a moment to answer and thinking over his words carefully. "I've been well. All things considered."

She nodded. "I want to offer my condolences again."

"Thank you," he said. "I got your card and flowers. That was very thoughtful."

She smiled. "We all chipped in a little." She leaned forward onto her desk and laced her fingers together. Without releasing them, she pointed to his papers which now rested on his lap. "Are you here to start work again, or has something else brought you in? A month off is company policy, but for you I can certainly make an exception."

He shifted in his chair. "Both, actually. I would like to resume work today, if you'll allow me."

She nodded, waiting for him to continue.

"But I've also come to give you my two weeks notice. I'm hoping you'll let me work for those two weeks."

"Of course. May I ask, what is pulling you away from the Daily World? I hope those biased weasels over at the National Inquiry aren't stealing you away from us."

He shook his head, placed the papers on her desk, and pushed them toward her.

She picked them up. He watched as her eyes scanned the pages, flipping one to the next. A smile slowly spread across her face, but the corners of her mouth betrayed a mixture of... Pain? Displeasure? He wasn't rightly sure.

"I suppose congratulations are in order," she said.

"Thank you."

"The United States Navy. And you'll be leaving for training in..."

"Two weeks and two days," he finished for her. "But I've still got to eat in that time."

She nodded and set the papers down. "Are you sure this what you want to do? Support to keep the U.S. out of the war has been draining every month. And that war... it's unlike anything this world has ever seen."

He nodded. "I've given it a good deal of thought. I've always thought the life of a sailor, well... it has always appealed to me. Only, I wouldn't have ever gone when my mother—" his voice choked off.

It caught him by surprise, the sudden wave of grief washing over him. He struggled to find words, but Ms. Hudson stepped in for him.

She smiled gently and more genuinely this time. "You've got only one life to live. And if this is what you want... well, you're in the prime of your youth. You deserve to chase your dreams."

He nodded. "Thank you."

She shuffled the papers and handed them back to him. He folded them into thirds and slipped them into a pocket of his vest. "I'll see to the paperwork on our end. Should you ever find yourself in civilian life again, you'll be welcome back here."

Henry nodded. He hoped it wouldn't come to that. The Navy would give him training on other things, things that might enable him to have a real career somewhere down the road.

"Thank you," he said. "That's a generous offer. And I really appreciate your understanding in all of this."

"Of course. We all want the best for you, Henry. Just stay safe, okay?"

Henry checked his watch. "Fifteen minutes 'til I need to clock in. If you don't mind, I'd like to get an early start on the day."

She smiled at him. "Of course."

As he left her office, he felt the papers rustle under his vest. He clutched at them over his clothes, making sure they were still there.

He'd be on his way soon enough.

14

In mid-afternoon, Henry sat on his stool next to a pile of newspapers ready to be sold. He watched as people came and went.

It was remarkable, how they all had these individual lives. They all had problems, heartaches, bills, and dreams.

His moods had proven unpredictable. He bounced between sudden grief and uncontrollable excitement. He was looking forward to training. And he felt certain the time away from Des Moines would help clear his head.

The next year seemed impossibly hopeful, even with the possibility of war.

He was lost in watching the people mull about their days as a familiar voice called his name.

"Henry!"

He looked over his shoulder to see Jeff Anderson jogging up to him with a bouquet of flowers in his hand.

He smiled. "Hello, there, Mr. Anderson." Henry gestured to the flowers. "You should know, I prefer roses, sir."

Mr. Anderson laughed. "I'll keep that in mind. Daisies are my wife's favorite."

"Well, that's very thoughtful of you, sir."

Mr. Anderson nodded, and his face changed to a frown. "I haven't seen you around for a while. I did a bit of asking around, and I'm very sorry to hear about your mother. You have our deepest condolences."

"Thank you, sir. She passed away peacefully, which is all we can really hope for in the end I suppose."

Mr. Anderson nodded. "That's very wise of you. Have you been back to work long?"

"About a week now, sir," Henry said.

Mr. Anderson nodded. "I'm not working in this neighborhood anymore, so I'm not sure how often I'll get to see you."

"Is that so?" Henry said. "Where are you at now?"

"The Prime Selections office," Mr. Anderson replied. "I took up a position there. Tri-City Director of Sales."

Henry slapped his knee. "Well, fancy that! That's wonderful news. Congratulations, sir."

Mr. Anderson looked a bit bashful. "Thank you. You know, you should come over for supper some time. My boys would get a kick out of your riddles. And Lynn would love to meet the man that sold me the paper that got me my new job."

"I'd love that. It's very kind of you to offer. We'll need to make it happen sooner rather than later. I'll be leaving town in about a week."

"Leaving town? Where you headed off to?"

Henry sat up a little straighter. "Training. I've enlisted with the United States Navy."

Mr. Anderson smiled broadly, but Henry noticed the same downturn at the corners of his mouth that Ms. Hudson had shown him. "Well, congratulations! That's a big change. You sure that's the right thing to do, what with the world in the state it's in?"

Henry held up a hand to stop him. "I've given it a lot of thought. And nearly everybody has the same concerns. Even my pastor was a bit worried over it. But yes, I'm sure. I've only got one life to live. And I've known for a good while now that a life of service is what's best suited for me."

Mr. Anderson cocked his head and pursed his lips. "That's... that's very noble of you. And for a man of your age, well... it must be the honest truth."

"Thank you, sir. And to tell truth upon truth, I'm really excited for it."

"Good," Mr. Anderson said. "Well, listen. I've got to get these flowers home so Lynn can put them in a vase. I'll talk to her about dinner and come back tomorrow. Are you working tomorrow?"

"Yes, sir. I am."

"Perfect. I'll make sure she's alright with it, and we'll get it taken care of. Sound good to you?"

"That sounds wonderful. A home-cooked meal would do me good."

"It's a plan, then." Mr. Anderson began walking back the way he'd come when Henry called out to him.

"Mr. Anderson? You forgot your paper."

15

Henry had never spent Thanksgiving in Iowa City, but it had been a year for change.

Aunt Rose had successfully sold the old house in August. Visiting her on his week of leave made the most sense.

Henry stood in her kitchen, and the myriad of smells assaulted his hunger. A brined and sage-adorned turkey roasted in the oven.

Aunt Rose was just a little heavier than most women with short, red hair painfully sculpted into tight curls. Her three daughters, Amelia, Mary, and Florence, busied themselves around the table, getting it set for dinner.

Uncle Thomas sat on the couch, grumbling over his newspaper and casting angry glances up at the radio.

"Are you sure I can't help, Aunt Rose?" Henry asked.

Busy at the stove, she shook her head to shoo him away.

He shrugged. The girls were moving so rapidly around the table, he knew he'd be more of a hindrance than a help there.

He sank down onto the sofa with Uncle Thomas.

"I don't believe you ever paid me for your cab ride back," Uncle Thomas said.

Henry gaped at him, but he dug into his pockets. He pulled out a couple of dollar bills and some change.

He noticed that among them was the 1910 penny, the miss-stamped one, that had come from Mr. Anderson. He'd kept it all throughout his basic training. That seemed like a lifetime ago.

"It was two dollars and fifty-eight cents," Uncle Thomas growled.

Henry handed him $2.75. He kept the sentimental penny and placed his remaining change back into his pocket.

Uncle Thomas looked up at him, and a glint of contempt sparked in his eyes. "This is your military's fault, I hope you know."

"Sorry?" Henry said. "What's their fault?"

Uncle Thomas jabbed his newspaper toward the silent radio. "A Thanksgiving with war looming!" He pointed a stubby finger at him. "I hope your enlistment means this whole business with the Germans and those Axis-whomevers comes to an end sooner."

Henry leaned away from his Uncle. "Serving in the armed forces is an important pursuit, Uncle."

Uncle Thomas chuffed. "Oh, a right noble cause. Go get yourself shipped out to heaven-knows-where, fighting heathens or fascists or whatever flag they're flying."

"Henry, I think I could use your help in here after all," Aunt Rose called.

Henry quickly fled the couch and came to her aid.

She lowered her voice to a whisper. "I don't really need help. I just wanted to get you away from him."

"Thank you," he said. "I didn't want to get into a real argument with him."

She went to the stove, and he stood at her side with his back toward the living room. "Sorry. He's been very cranky. He thinks Thanksgiving is about nothing more than food—that he never helps with, I might add."

Henry smiled at her. "I'll just busy myself around here and try to stay out of your way."

It was Henry who carved the turkey as the girls placed bowls and platters at the table. Once everything was ready, they all sat down to eat.

Uncle Thomas said grace, albeit in a mumbling, angry tone and very hastily.

Conversation drifted as they ate. The girls talked about school, and music lessons. Aunt Rose updated everyone on the latest family gossip, and what the neighbors were up to, and what the church was planning to do around Christmas.

Uncle Thomas gave a barely audible response of either *yes*, *no*, or *I don't know* to any question bold enough to venture his way.

"Will you be home for Christmas?" Aunt Rose asked Henry.

"No, I don't expect so," he said.

"You haven't told us yet where you're being deployed to," she said.

He wiped his mouth with his napkin. "It's quite exciting. I was hoping to share the news over the meal."

All three girls stilled their forks to stare at him. Aunt Rose sat up a little straighter. Uncle Thomas kept his head tilted toward his plate, but his eyes at least moved upward.

It had been exactly the type of assignment Henry had hoped for. A chance to see the world outside of Iowa. "I've been assigned to the U.S.S. California at the Naval Station Pearl Harbor in Hawaii."

16

Henry had been fighting to sleep all night.

He restlessly watched as the clock on the wall ticked later and later into the morning.

The other men in his bunk didn't seem to suffer the way he did. Lazy snores and the noise of deep breaths resounded through the ship's cabin.

7:49am.

Henry supposed he should get up, should head out for breakfast in preparation for his shift. His stomach rumbled.

The food on the ship wasn't amazing, but he'd certainly endured worse, especially during the lean days of his mother's illness.

His stomach lurched, this time with nausea. He just couldn't shake the uneasy feeling in his gut that something big, something imminent was approaching.

He rolled over to face the wall. He'd stuck up a couple pictures, including the one of that fishing trip so many years ago. He didn't have many pictures of his father. And that one was his favorite.

He lay there for a few minutes, recalling the joy of that day, trying to recapture those emotions and put his mind at ease.

Then he heard it.

A loud, deep boom. The scream of metal yanking apart, the rush of fire and sky ripping open nearby.

He jerked upright.

Another boom sounded, louder than the last. Closer.

Other men began rising from their sleep, looking around for the source of the noise.

Another boom.

Then another.

Henry tore off his pajamas and dove for his uniform. Everyone was awake now and following his lead.

Another boom, but this one rocked the California. The roar of breaking metal around Henry was deafening. The ship vaulted violently, rocking them back and forth, sending men and possessions flying.

An angry, urgent voice came over the loudspeaker. "ALL HANDS TO GENERAL QUARTERS. ALL HANDS TO GENERAL QUARTERS. THIS IS NOT A DRILL. WE ARE UNDER ATTACK. ALL HANDS TO GENERAL QUARTERS."

The 1910 penny jingled in the pocket of his pants as he yanked them on to run to his battle station.

ACKNOWLEDGMENTS

I want to thank my family and especially my sister, Dr. Cynthia Reynolds-Temple, who encouraged me to finish this book.

I also want to thank the Lord for providing for my family and me.

ABOUT THE AUTHOR

Curt Reynolds is Director of Logistics for a food manufacturing company in the Sheboygan Falls, WI area and is a graduate of Iowa State University.

Curt serves on The Board of Directors of The Mentor Corps in Minneapolis, MN. He previously served as Chairman of The Twin Cities Salvation Army Advisory Board in Minneapolis, MN.

He lives in Wisconsin with his wife and daughter.

Made in the USA
Monee, IL
15 December 2019